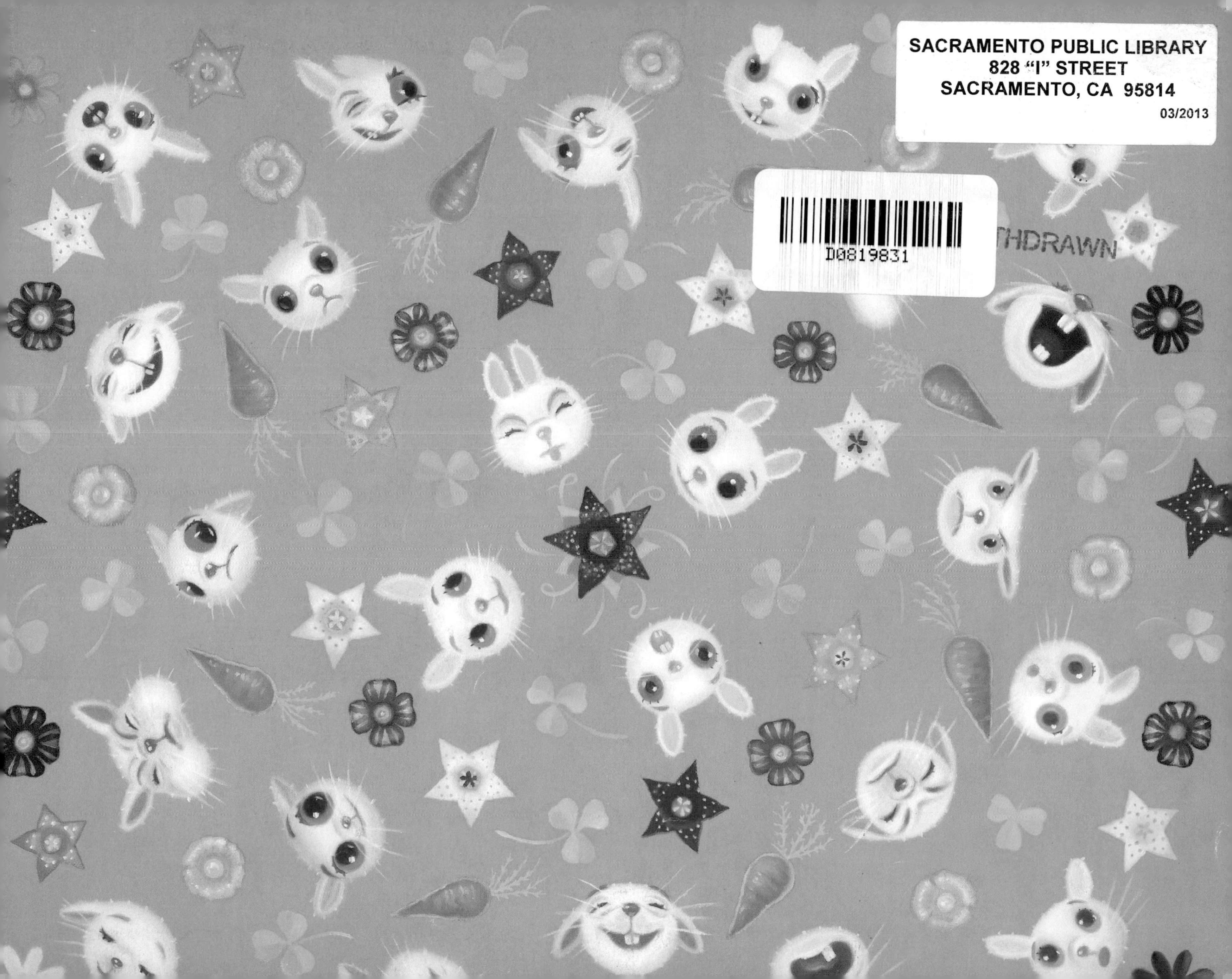

To my oh so tiny bunnies,
Primrose and Wisteria.

A FEIWEL AND FRIENDS BOOK
An Imprint of Macmillan

Library of Congress Cataloging-in-Publication Data Available

ISBN: 978-1-250-01688-1

Feiwel and Friends logo designed by Filomena Tuosto
The artwork was created with oils on paper.

First Edition: 2013

10 9 8 7 6 5 4 3 2

mackids.com

OH SO TINY BUNNY

story and paintings by

David Kirk

FEIWEL AND FRIENDS

NEW YORK

Oh So Tiny is a very small bunny—

with very big dreams.

His dreams are SO big, you might
not think they could squeeze
into a bunny so small.

When Oh So sleeps,

he dreams that he is as big as a dragon,

as big as a forest,

as big as a mountain.

A bunny so very big, gets oh so very hungry.

So he dreams of sweet clover as
tall as trees,

of crunchy carrots as big as railroad cars, and fields of lettuce as wide as oceans.

Is something missing from Oh So's dreams?

He needs a friend to play with.

Are there no other bunnies so big as Oh So?

He hops over houses.

He bounds over bridges.

He leaps over green hills and valleys.

But no matter where Oh So looks . . .

there is no bunny.

Oh So feels, oh so very lonely.

And his loneliness is SO big.

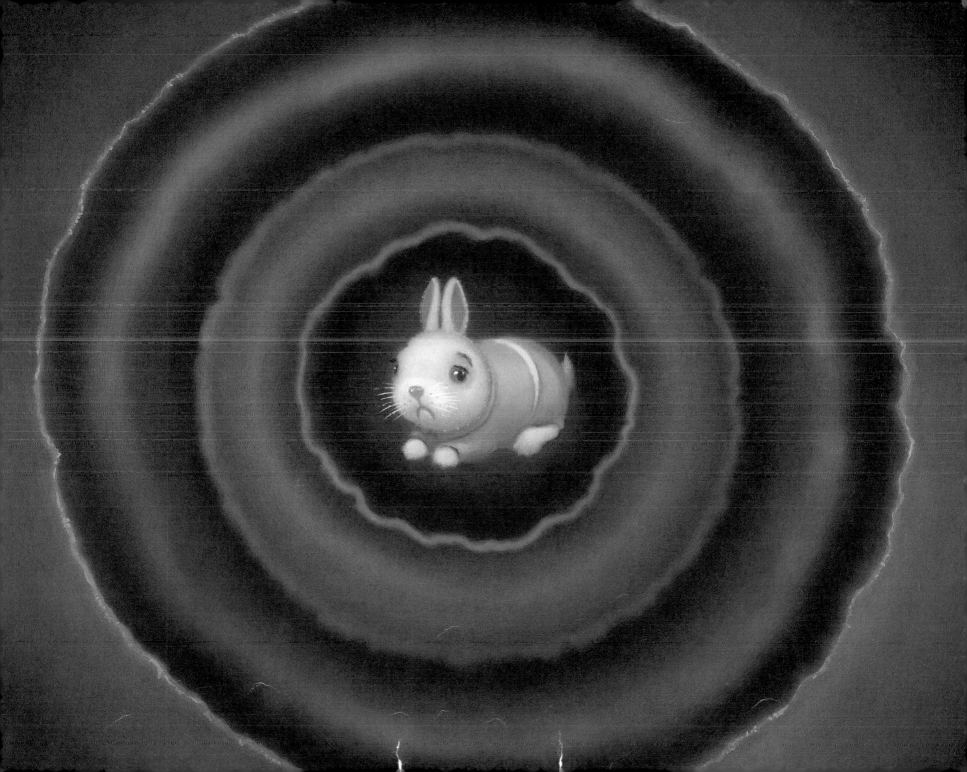

But wait! Oh So feels a nibble on his ear.

He shakes himself awake.

Good morning, little bunny.

Sometimes, thinks Oh So . . .

it's better to be small.